For Friedrich Neugebauer in celebration of his 90th birthday, November 2001

Lisbeth Zwerger

Copyright © 2002 by Michael Neugebauer Verlag, an imprint of Nord-Süd Verlag AG, Gossau Zürich, Switzerland
First published in Switzerland under the title Schwanensee.
English translation copyright © 2002 by North-South Books Inc., New York

First published in the United States, Great Britain, Canada,
Australia, and New Zealand in 2002 by North-South Books,
an imprint of Nord-Süd Verlag AG, Gossau Zürich, Switzerland.

Distributed in the United States by North-South Books Inc., New York.

Library of Congress Cataloging-in-Publication Data is available.
A CIP catalogue record for this book is available from The British Library.
ISBN 0-7358-1702-2 (trade edition) 10 9 8 7 6 5 4 3 2 1
ISBN 0-7358-1703-0 (library edition) 10 9 8 7 6 5 4 3 2 1
Printed in Italy

For more information about our books, and the authors and artists
who create them, visit our web site: www.northsouth.com

Swan Lake

By Pyotr I. Tchaikovsky
Retold and illustrated by
Lisbeth Zwerger

Translated by Marianne Martens

A Michael Neugebauer Book
North-South Books · New York/London

Once upon a time, all you needed was the right mix of enough evil and a good spell to transform a person into a tree, a rock, or even an animal. In those days, there lived a prince. He was still very young, and he thought that life was all about enjoying himself. He spent his days dreaming and playing, and he spent his nights going to party after party. The prince was very happy and had absolutely no desire to change anything.

On the night before his eighteenth birthday, the prince invited some of his friends to a big party. There was dancing under the trees in the castle garden, and everyone was having a wonderful time with girls from the village. But the prince's mother was not pleased with her son. Not one bit.

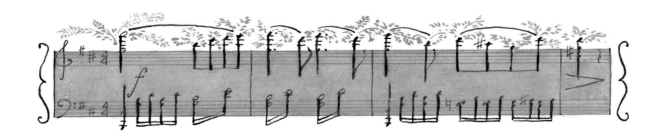

"My dear son," she said, "how will this end? You are practically grown up, and yet you still have no wife! Tomorrow we will throw a ball and invite many princesses. You shall choose one of them to marry."

The prince was surprised, but he wasn't worried. "Tomorrow is still far away," he said to himself. "I won't let that ruin the evening."

Just then, the air rustled as a flock of wild swans flew over the heads of the guests.

"Come!" the prince called to his friends. "Let's go hunting!"

Armed with bows and arrows, they raced after the large birds, shooting their arrows high into the sky, but they could barely keep up with the swans whose feathers glowed bright in the darkness. Suddenly the prince felt a little dizzy. So while his friends continued the chase, he stayed behind to rest by the lake.

With a flash, the lake was bathed in a shimmering light, and before him stood the most
beautiful woman he had ever seen.

"Who are you?" asked the prince.

She jumped, startled at his voice, and stared nervously at his bow and arrows. It wasn't until
he put them aside that she spoke. "I am the Swan Queen," she said. "I am the swan that you
tried to kill."

"How can that be?" asked the prince.

She told him her tragic tale. An evil sorcerer had transformed her and her friends into swans.
Every night at midnight, she could take her human form again, but at dawn she always
turned back into a swan. The Swan Queen sighed, "Only one thing can release me from this
spell—the true love of a man."

"But then everything will be fine," said the prince, kneeling before her, "because I love you truly.
Only you, and no other."

He had barely finished speaking when, with a loud flapping, an owl flew through the air.
It was the evil sorcerer himself, who had taken the form of an owl to eavesdrop on the couple.
The prince begged the Swan Queen to come to the ball at the castle the next night, where
he would introduce her as his bride. Overjoyed, she agreed, and they held hands until dawn.
As the sun began to rise, a group of girls dressed in white hurried over. The prince watched in
amazement as the Swan Queen and her friends became birds once again.

The next night the castle had been gloriously decorated for the ball. The guests wore their most elegant clothes. All the princesses had done everything they could to make themselves look beautiful. Tonight the prince was going to choose his bride, and each one wanted to be chosen.

Pale-faced, the prince stood next to his mother and greeted the guests. More and more princesses were presented to him. Each one danced for him, but the prince found it all very tiresome. After every dance, his mother said, "Well, my son?" But the prince only thought of his beloved Swan Queen.

Suddenly the lights in the ballroom went out. The music stopped, and the dancers froze.
All eyes turned to the huge French doors where, amid thunder and lightning, new guests
arrived—a prince and his beautiful daughter, both dressed all in black.
"At last! At last you are here!" cried the prince.
He ran up to the great beauty and kissed her hands. She seemed different somehow. Her black
clothing and her haughty bearing confused him, but nonetheless he turned to his mother and
declared, "This is the woman that I love, and that I will love forever. Only her, and no other."

The sound of his words was still in the air when the French doors opened once again. A woman in a radiant white dress entered. It was the Swan Queen.

Alas—she had seen it all. The prince, who only the night before had professed his eternal love to her, held another woman in his arms! Betrayed, the Swan Queen fled sobbing from the castle.

Immediately, the prince realized that he had been tricked. The woman he held in his arms was a stranger. Nothing about her reminded him of his love. And taking a closer look, he saw that her father had some rather owl-like features. The Black Prince was none other than the sorcerer himself!

In anguish, the prince raced after his Swan Queen. He feared that everything was lost, yet hoped he could somehow save her.

Beside himself with sorrow and anger he ran through the dark forest to the lake. And there he found her, surrounded by her friends.

When the girls saw the prince approaching, they gathered in a protective circle around their queen. But what did they know about love? Just seconds before, the Swan Queen had been complaining bitterly about the fickleness of her prince—had sworn to be rid of him forever. And now she ran to him with open arms.

"Whatever happens," said the prince, "I will stay by your side. My love for you is stronger than anything. No danger will chase me away."

At his words, great waves appeared on the lake. The water rose higher and higher, flooding the banks. The Swan Queen was pulled into the water.

The sorcerer's evil power was indeed great. But greater yet was the power of love. . . .

Some believe that in the final battle the prince stabbed the sorcerer. Others insist that the prince jumped into the lake after his love, and they drowned together. Still others are convinced that they are living at the bottom of the lake in a paradise of eternal joy.

But the truth is that the prince saved the Swan Queen from the sorcerer's flood, and thus the evil spell was broken.

The prince introduced his true love to his mother, and soon after they were married. The bridesmaids were reluctant to wear white dresses with feather trim—and who could blame them? Instead they wore green, and the bride wore an elegant silk gown of the palest pink. The prince and princess had a long and happy life together.

There are people who can watch ROMEO AND JULIET over and over again and still hope for a happy ending each time. I belong to this group of people.

So it was with mixed feelings that I began work on the beautiful story of SWAN LAKE. Once I started work on the project, however, I was very relieved to learn its history.

In 1871 Pyotr Ilich Tchaikovsky, who was thirty-one years old at the time, wrote a one-act fairy-tale dance piece. He wrote it for the children of his sister, Alexandra Davydova, and named it SWAN LAKE. Four years later, he received a commission from the Moscow Theater to make a ballet of the same title.

SWAN LAKE is the best-loved ballet of all time, but when it premiered in 1877, it was anything but successful. No one knows exactly why it was such a disaster. Apparently, some considered the choreography to be undanceable. The prima ballerina felt that she wasn't being challenged and insisted on inserting solos from other ballets. Because of this, the piece lost its overall harmony and the story suffered.

It is also not clear who the actual author of the libretto was. Tchaikovsky may have written it himself. The basic themes of SWAN LAKE can be found in the world of the German fairy tale, but Richard Wagner's LOHENGRIN and Ludwig II, the fairy-tale king of Bavaria, also inspired the author.

Sixteen years after its premiere, and one year after Tchaikovsky's death in 1893, the score and the choreography were drastically changed. Tchaikovsky's brother, Modest, reworked the libretto. But the biggest change was that the story was now given a tragic ending. In the original, Tchaikovsky had let love conquer evil.

You can imagine how relieved I was to find this. Since Tchaikovsky himself had wanted a happy ending for SWAN LAKE, I felt free to do the same. The other big relief for me was to omit the names of the main characters—Siegfried, Odette, Odile—that always seemed foreign to me. For this suggestion, and also for several beautiful sentences, I am grateful to Heinz Janisch. I thank Susanne Koppe for her sensitive editing.

Lisbeth Zwerger, September 2001